Hello, Family Members,

Learning to read is one of the most importan~~t accomplishmen~~ of early childhood. **Hello Reader!** books are designed to help children become skilled readers who like to read. Beginning readers learn to read by remembering frequently used words like "the," "is," and "and"; by using phonics skills to decode new words; and by interpreting picture and text clues. These books provide both the stories children e~~njoy and the structure they need to read~~ fluently and independe~~ntly~~ ld *before*,

during, a~~nd~~

- Look at ~~~~ ict
  what th~~~~
- Read th~~~~
- Encour~~~~
  and phr~~~~
- Echo re~~~~ ving
  your ch~~~~

- Have yo~~~~
  recogni~~~~ we
  know th~~~~ his
  one?"
- Encour~~~~ new
  words.
- Provide~~~~
  needed ~~~~ ience
  of readi~~~~
- Encour~~~~ of
  express~~~~

- Have y~~~~ rds.
- Encour~~~~ ain.
  Have h~~~~
  and ev~~~~ ence
  in your~~~~
- Talk ab~~~~ s and
  ideas a~~~~
  events ~~~~

I do hope

For amazing Mavis
—K.M.

To Mike and Mikaela — Sweet Dreams
—M.S.

ISBN 0-439-31945-5

Text copyright © 2003 by Kate McMullan.
Illustrations copyright © 2003 by Mavis Smith.
All rights reserved. Published by Scholastic Inc.
SCHOLASTIC, HELLO READER, CARTWHEEL BOOKS, and associated logos are trademarks and/or registered trademarks of Scholastic Inc.

Library of Congress Cataloging-in-Publication Data
McMullan, Kate.
    Fluffys plants a jelly bean / by Kate McMullan ; illustrated by Mavis Smith.
        p. cm. — (Hello reader! Level 3)
    Summary: After Fluffy the guinea pig buries a jelly bean in the school yard, he dreams that he is Fluffy Jack in a story about a jelly bean stalk and a giant.
    ISBN 0-439-31945-5
        [1. Guinea pigs — Fiction. 2. Dreams — Fiction. 3. Jelly beans — Fiction. 4. Giants — Fiction. 5. Schools — Fiction.] I. Smith, Mavis, ill. II. Title. III. Series.
PZ7.M47879 Fldk 2003
[E] — dc21

10 9 8 7 6 5 4 3   03 04 05 06 07
            Printed in the U.S.A. 24 • First printing, March 2003

FLUFFY
PLANTS A JELLY BEAN

by Kate McMullan
Illustrated by Mavis Smith

Hello Reader! — Level 3

SCHOLASTIC INC.

Cartwheel
B·O·O·K·S ®

New York   Toronto   London   Auckland   Sydney
Mexico City   New Delhi   Hong Kong   Buenos Aires

Fluffy Plants a Jelly Bean

"Have some sunflower seeds, Fluffy,"
said Wade.
Fluffy dove into his bowl.
He started cracking the shells
and eating the seeds.
Yum! thought Fluffy.

Sunflower seeds stuck to Fluffy's face.

They stuck to his ears.

They stuck to his paws and to his fur.

But he did not mind the mess.

I love sunflower seeds! thought Fluffy.

Emma picked Fluffy up. She put him
in a basket and took him outside.
"We are having an egg hunt," she said.
"You can hunt for eggs with us."
Yes! thought Fluffy. **I am a good hunter!**

"Here's a yellow egg!" said Wade.
He put it into his basket.
"Here's one with blue stripes!" said Emma.
She put her basket down and reached
under a bush to get the egg.
Time to go hunting! thought Fluffy.
He jumped out of the basket.

Fluffy thought he saw a bright green egg.

He picked it up.

He put it into the basket.

"That's not an egg, Fluffy," said Emma.

"That's a jelly bean."

A bean? thought Fluffy. **I love beans!**

Fluffy thought back to last spring.
Ms. Day's class had planted a garden.
The kids planted beans.
Big bean plants grew from the beans.
Lots of little beans grew
from the plants.

Now spring had come again.

Now Fluffy had a bright green bean.

I will grow a bean plant! he thought.

Fluffy ran over to the class garden.

The soil had been turned over.

But nothing had been planted yet.

Fluffy dug a little hole.

He dropped the bright green bean

into the hole and covered it with dirt.

You're planted now, bean! thought Fluffy.

"Fluffy planted a jelly bean!" said Wade.

"Fluffy!" said Emma. "That won't grow!"

Yes, it will, thought Fluffy. **It is a bean.**

Beans grow into bean plants.

I know my bean will grow!

Fluffy Jack and the Jelly Bean Stalk

It was almost summer. After lunch,
Ms. Day opened all the windows.
She read the class a story.
Fluffy closed his eyes and listened.
Once upon a time, read Ms. Day,
a poor widow needed money to buy food.
So she sent her son ...

. . . Fluffy Jack to sell the cow.
"How much money did you get?"
his mother asked when he came home.
"No money!" said Fluffy Jack.
"I sold the cow for magic jelly beans."

"Magic jelly beans?" cried his mother.

"Phooey!" She threw them out the window.

"Maybe they will grow," said Fluffy Jack.

"They won't grow!" said his mother.

That night Fluffy Jack looked out the
window. He saw a big green stalk shoot
out of the ground. It grew right where
the magic jelly beans had landed.
"I knew they would grow," said Fluffy Jack.

Fluffy Jack ran outside.

He began to climb the jelly bean stalk.

Up, up, up he went.

At last, Fluffy Jack came to a land
above the clouds. He saw a big castle.
He walked up to the door and slipped inside.

Fluffy Jack saw a giant!
He was holding a little hen.
"Lay me a golden egg!" said the giant.
"No way!" said the hen.
The giant put the hen down.

The giant sniffed the air. He yelled,
"FEE-FI-FO-FIGGY!
I SMELL THE BLOOD OF A GUINEA PIGGY!
AND I'M GOING TO EAT HIM UP!"
Fluffy Jack jumped into a flowerpot and hid.

At last the giant fell asleep.
Fluffy Jack hopped out of the pot.
He picked up the hen and ran
to the jelly bean stalk.

Fluffy Jack climbed down the jelly bean stalk.
He gave the hen to his mother.
"Have a golden egg," said the hen.
"Wow!" said Fluffy Jack's mother. "Thanks!"

The next night, Fluffy Jack climbed up
the jelly bean stalk again.
He went into the giant's castle.
Now the giant had a golden harp.
"Play 'Pop Goes the Weasel'!" said the giant.
"Not again!" said the harp.

The giant sniffed the air. He yelled,
"FEE-FI-FO-FIGGY!
I SMELL THE BLOOD OF A GUINEA PIGGY!
AND I'M GOING TO EAT HIM UP!"
Fluffy Jack dove into the flowerpot again.
He hid until the giant fell asleep.

The giant began to snore.
Fluffy Jack hopped out of the pot.
He picked up the harp, ran to the
jelly bean stalk, and climbed down.

Fluffy Jack gave the harp to his mother.
"Would you like to hear 'Jelly Bean Rock'?"
said the harp.
"I love that song!" said Fluffy Jack's mother.
"Me, too," said the hen.

The next night, Fluffy Jack climbed up
the jelly bean stalk again. He pushed open
the door of the castle. But this time,
the giant was waiting for him.

"Yikes!" said Fluffy Jack.
"YIKES IS RIGHT!" said the giant.
"I'M GOING TO MAKE ME
A GUINEA PIGGY PIE!"

Fluffy Jack ran back
to the jelly bean stalk.
He slid down so fast
his pants were smoking.
"Help!" he called. "The giant is after me!"

"Get the axe and chop down the stalk!"
said the hen.
"We don't have an axe,"
said Fluffy Jack's mother.
The giant was climbing down fast!

"Get the saw and saw down the stalk!"
said the harp.
"We don't have a saw,"
said Fluffy Jack's mother.
The giant was almost down!
"Uh-oh!" said Fluffy Jack.

Fluffy Jack began to chew
on the jelly bean stalk.
He chewed and chewed.
The stalk began to wobble.

But the giant was climbing quickly.
One big foot was about to touch the ground.
Fluffy Jack chewed faster.
The giant was coming!
He had to chew faster!
And faster!
And faster!

Get Me Out of Here!

"Wake up, Fluffy!" said Emma.

Huh? thought Fluffy.

"Look at your chew stick," said Wade.

"You chewed it in your sleep!"

Chew stick? thought Fluffy.

Emma picked Fluffy up.

"You were dreaming," she said.

Whew! thought Fluffy.

Then there is no jelly bean stalk!

"We have a surprise for you, Fluffy,"
said Wade.

Oh, boy, said Fluffy.

I could use a carrot right now.

Wade and Emma took Fluffy outside.
They walked over to the class garden.
Lots of things were growing now.
Fluffy saw plants with string beans
and lima beans.
Where is my surprise? thought Fluffy.

Emma pointed to a sunflower.
It had big green leaves.
It had a thick stalk.

"Do you see that tall plant, Fluffy?"
said Emma. "It's growing right where
you planted the jelly bean," said Wade.

Fluffy stared at the tall plant.
Yikes! thought Fluffy. **My bean
really grew! But who cares?**

Get me out of here!